Mama
Had to Work
–on–
Christmas

BY Carolyn Marsden
ILLUSTRATIONS BY Robert Casilla

Viking

VIKING

Published by Penguin Group

Penguin Young Readers Group, 345 Hudson Street, New York, New York 10014, U.S.A.

Penguin Books Ltd, 80 Strand, London WC2R ORL, England

Penguin Books Australia Ltd, 250 Camberwell Road, Camberwell, Victoria 3124, Australia

Penguin Books Canada Ltd, 10 Alcorn Avenue, Toronto, Ontario, Canada M4V 3B2

Penguin Books (N.Z.) Ltd, 182-190 Wairau Road, Auckland 10, New Zealand

Published in 2003 by Viking, a division of Penguin Young Readers Group

1 3 5 7 9 10 8 6 4 2

Text copyright © Carolyn Marsden, 2003

Illustrations copyright © Robert Casilla, 2003

LIBRARY OF CONGRESS CATALOGING-IN-PUBLICATION DATA

Marsden, Carolyn.

Mama had to work on Christmas / by Carolyn Marsden.

p. cm.

Summary: Gloria's Christmas begins with frustration when she is forced
to go to work with Mama, but by the end of the day, she appreciates her family
and enjoys the holiday.

ISBN 0-670-03635-8

[1. Christmas—Fiction. 2. Work—Fiction. 3. Mexican
Americans—Fiction.] I. Title.

PZ7.M35135Mam 2003   [Fic]—dc21   2003000943

Printed in U.S.A.

Set in Garamond, Schow

Book design by Teresa Kietlinski

I would like to acknowledge my editor, Melanie Cecka,
for her hard work, encouragement, and faith in this story. —C.M.

For my daughters,
Maleeka Vayna and Preeyanutt Manita;
my loving husband, Panratt;
my mother, Winifred;
and the Hispanic community
which made this story possible.
—C. M.

For my daughter Emily,
who loves Christmas.
—R.C.

❦

Contents

CHAPTER 1

A Dark Christmas Morning

"Merry Christmas, Gloria!"

Gloria opened her eyes to see Mama wearing her pink uniform with her name tag pinned above the pocket. Why did Mama look as though she was going to work?

"Wake up, Gloria. I have something to tell you, *mija*."

Gloria's whole sleepy body woke up.

"The hotel just called. Rosalinda is sick and I have to take her place. You'll have to come with me."

"Why, Mama?"

"Because Papi is away working."

"But Mama, tell them no! It's *Christmas*!" Gloria turned over in bed. First Papi had to

1

work on Christmas, now Mama. She didn't want to see that uniform.

"If I tell them no, *mija,* I'll lose my job."

"But we're supposed to go to Nana's."

"We'll go later, tonight."

Gloria lay down again and turned her face into the pillow. The pillow pressed against her lips as she said, "Can't you take me to Nana's first?"

Mama sighed. "You know that would take too long."

"But she's so close by!" Gloria could see Nana's *colonia* from the top of the slide on the school playground. Nana's house was perched somewhere on that hill. Gloria and Nana had promised to wave toward each other, from two different countries, every day during lunch recess.

"She's still too far." Mama walked away and Gloria snuggled deeper into the covers. She'd looked forward to going to Nana's even though Papi wouldn't be there.

Papi usually picked flowers along with

other workers. They were called *migrant*, Papi explained, because they moved to whatever crop needed to be picked. Sometimes Papi came home with his sleeves smelling like carnations, a clove scent that reminded Gloria of the cakes that Mama baked. Papi described fields of flowers taller than Gloria.

Sometimes Gloria imagined running down the rows of bright, sweet flowers, her clothes covered with golden pollen.

Papi usually had Sundays and holidays off. But this Christmas, because of the sudden cold weather, all of the migrant workers had been ordered to move from the flower fields to the neighboring orange grove to harvest oranges before the freeze. During emergencies Papi had to sleep in a green canvas tent near the oranges. It made Gloria sad to think of Papi sleeping on a hard cot. She missed kissing his scratchy, whiskery cheek.

Last Christmas they'd had a barbecue at the beach near Nana's house. It had been Gloria's idea. Papi had brought his shovel and dug a deep pit. Gloria had wadded up newspaper. After Papi piled on some sticks, Gloria had showed him where to light the fire, here and there, all around.

"What a brave little fire," Nana had remarked, and Gloria had thought so, too. All day long, the flames flashed happily—red, yellow, orange—in spite of the cold wind.

Gloria had run back and forth as the waves chased her. When they caught her, she screamed with delight.

Mama pulled the covers off Gloria. "Enough!" she said.

So Gloria got up and pulled on a skirt and blouse and sweater.

Missy, her doll, needed to be dressed, too. Missy couldn't be left alone on Christmas. Gloria checked Missy's blond hair, tucked a few strands into place, then straightened Missy's pink-striped dress.

"Will we come back before Nana's?" Gloria called to Mama.

"We won't have time."

So Gloria brought out the shopping bag that had been hidden deep in her closet. Inside were the gifts that she'd worked hard at school to make. There was a huge pinecone with glitter on it for Papi, a plaster-of-paris handprint painted red for Mama, and a clay angel for Nana's Nativity. The angel was wrapped in many layers of tissue paper so that the wings and halo wouldn't break off.

Gloria had looked forward to giving the presents. For weeks, she'd imagined everyone's looks of happiness as they held up the treasures. Gloria sighed. This year one thing after another was going wrong.

❧

"But it's still nighttime," Gloria protested.

Mama pulled the front door shut several times, trying to line the lock up. "The hotel is far away and buses don't run often on Christmas," Mama replied as they began their walk to the bus stop. "Let me carry your shopping bag."

They passed the warehouses where trucks loaded and unloaded wooden chests carved with flowers, racks of dresses, and big wheels of wire. This morning, all was quiet, the buildings fastened shut with padlocks.

As they passed Sandra's house, Gloria slowed down and walked way behind Mama. Sandra was her best friend at school. The lights were on in the house. Someone was probably stuffing a Christmas piñata with goodies.

Old cars crouched around Sandra's yard like huge sleeping animals. Sandra's uncles and cousins slept in them whenever they came over from Mexico looking for jobs. The cars were like extra bedrooms. Sandra and Gloria picked the wildflowers that grew around the wheels, chewing the stems, the yellow petals dangling from their mouths. The men would lean out the windows to say hi. Gloria and Sandra always said hi back.

"Can't I stay with Sandra?" Gloria asked.

"It's too early to call. Besides, it's Christmas and there's too many people at Sandra's already."

They arrived at the bus stop and sat down on the bench. Gloria counted stars as they

waited, watching them go out one by one as the sky turned a pale green.

Gloria wiggled her legs against each other to keep out the achy feeling.

Mama bent over and said, "Oh *mija*. Your little legs look so cold." Mama rubbed them quickly with the palms of her hands, up and down, until Gloria's skin glowed with warmth.

Her legs wouldn't have been cold if not for Mama. Gloria went to the other side of the bus bench. "Missy, we're at the North Pole. Let's find Santa." Gloria moved Missy's plastic legs back and forth, making her walk along the back of the bench. "See that big rock down there? That's Santa's bag of toys. He must have dropped it."

Missy tried to lift the rock, but it was too heavy.

"So many many toys," Gloria said as the bus approached, swinging along in the darkness.

The bus shrilled to a stop, then lurched once before the doors parted to let them in.

"Merry Christmas," the driver mumbled.

"Merry Christmas," Mama replied, then turned to Gloria. "See, *he's* working. Look. We have our choice of where to sit. Our own private limousine." She gestured toward the empty rows.

Gloria sat on a hard orange seat with Missy on her lap. She put her feet side by side on the slick metal floor.

Last year at the beach, Gloria had persuaded Mama and Nana to build a sand castle with her. Nana hiked up her long dress. Mama had played like a kid, searching for fronds of kelp for the castle flags. Gloria poked driftwood sticks around the castle for a fence. Papi used the shovel to dig a moat that filled with water each time a wave washed high upon the sand.

Last year for Christmas, Gloria had gotten a camera. It was a real one, but disposable, so that it was no good after it had been used just once. At the beach, she'd shot the whole roll of film: Nana adding a log to the fire, Papi napping with a newspaper over his face, Mama sifting sand onto the sand castle. But Gloria had never seen the pictures.

"What happened to the film?" she'd asked around Valentine's Day.

"We can't afford to develop it right now," Papi had answered.

"What about the film?" Gloria had asked at Easter.

"There's too many bills to pay," Papi had said.

Gloria looked at her face reflected in the bus window, her black hair framing her cheeks. She tried to focus beyond herself, to the street with an occasional car, the headlights still on.

CHAPTER 2

On the Bus

For years, even before Gloria was born, Papi had worked in the flower fields. He rode an early morning bus like this one to work. At night, he came home smelling of damp earth and fertilizer. Soil always darkened the edges of his fingernails. Green from the leaves stained his clothes.

One time, he'd brought Gloria a long stem of orange-striped gladiolas, carrying it into the house like a wand.

"To work your magic, my princess," he said, bending down to hand it to her, his muddy fingers clutching the smooth stem.

Gloria had waved the flower back and forth in the air. "Our house is now a castle!"

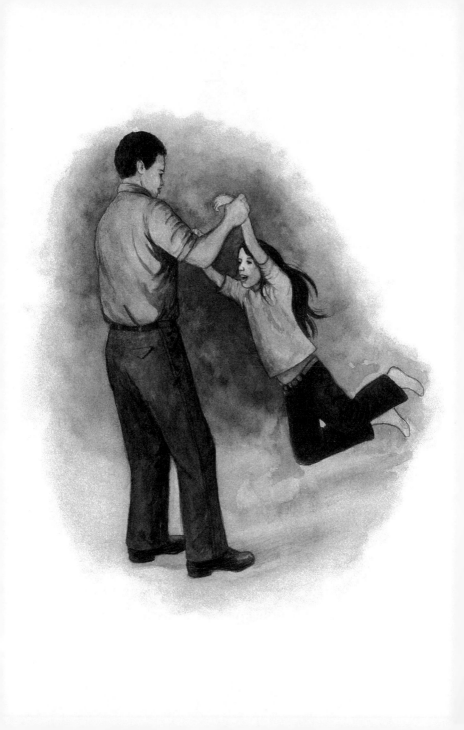

Papi had laughed, even though he looked so tired. He'd taken her by the forearms and swung her around and around in a circle so that her feet just missed touching the TV on one side of the room and the couch on the other. Then they both collapsed, dizzy, on the floor.

Gloria held Missy tighter. She wished that Papi didn't have to pick today. She glanced at Mama's reflection in the mirror of the bus. Her reflection was slippery in the bus window, the pink uniform waving back and forth.

Every morning Mama braided her hair, starting at the back of her head, then pulling the braid over one shoulder to finish up with quick fingers that snapped each strand of hair into place. Her cheeks were smooth and soft, her eyelashes long—she didn't need makeup to look pretty.

Mama loved to tell how she had marched right on into the fancy hotel and got the bathroom job. "I just told them that I was Marta Benitez, very capable, with a child to support.

Before I knew it, the woman was handing me bottles of cleaning fluid."

Gloria leaned against Mama's uniform that smelled like the sweet starch Mama sprayed as she ironed. She felt the wisps of Mama's hair against her cheek.

Last year at the beach they'd grilled hot dogs and eaten Nana's Christmas tamales.

As night fell, Nana had wrapped Gloria in a blanket and pulled her close.

"See there, Nana. That star there." Gloria pointed to the twinkle of light. "That's the one that guided the shepherds and wise men to the baby."

Last year they'd had the most perfect Christmas.

This year, Gloria wouldn't get to Nana's until Christmas was almost over.

The bus exited the freeway, curving along the off-ramp. As it turned, Gloria swayed away from Mama in her sweet-smelling uniform.

CHAPTER 3

The Biggest Christmas Tree

"Here we are," Mama announced as the bus slowed down. Gloria looked out to see another bus stopped in front of them. People in uniforms like Mama's were getting out.

"Merry Christmas," the driver said again.

"Merry Christmas," Mama said brightly, as though she had the whole day off. "Come on, Gloria. What are you staring at?"

Gloria stood on the bus steps where the doors fanned open. Mama had never told her the hotel was like *this.* The garden stretched as far as her eyes could see. Green lawns, a stream that wandered here and there, tiny bridges where the path crossed it. Red flowers bloomed like flames around the trunks of palm trees.

"Oh," was all Gloria could say as she stepped down to the sidewalk. Maybe being here all day wouldn't be so bad after all. "Just look, Missy," she whispered. "Even better than the beach."

They came to a large pool where seals sunbathed on the rocks. The seals lifted their snouts into the air and rocked back and forth on their flippers. Gloria imagined touching their glossy coats.

Mama went ahead. "Come on, *niña*. We'll be late."

Gloria didn't want to be late to the marvelous place that Mama was taking her.

As they walked quickly toward the hotel, Gloria tried to count the number of stories, tilting her head back until her neck hurt.

The inside of the building opened up into a gigantic bubble of a room. A Christmas tree bigger than any Gloria had ever dreamed of rose toward the ceiling. It must have come straight from a forest. When she breathed in, the sharp smell went all the way through her.

The tree was lit with lights and shiny balls. Gloria looked at herself in a red ball. Her cheeks grew huge, her forehead tiny. Such a funny face! "Jingle Bells" played softly in the background with the bells jingling as though real reindeer ran on the roof. For the first time that morning, Gloria felt warm all over.

The round tables were made of glass. Gloria wondered how it would feel to sit down and see her legs and feet underneath. She and Missy could play underwater games. They could play hide-and-seek around the pink couches with silver threads running through the fabric. A man sat alone on a couch, reading a newspaper, folding it apart and then back together again, as if he was no place special. A teenage boy in a uniform hurried through, pushing a cart piled high with suitcases.

Mama took Gloria by the arm and steered her across the thick pink carpet that still had the marks of the vacuum across it. Gloria wanted to lie down and press her whole body against the softness.

They stepped into an elevator. As it rose, Gloria's stomach grew heavy.

When the elevator jerked to a halt, the doors slid open to reveal a sign that said LADIES.

CHAPTER 4

WET FLOORS

When Mama opened the door to the bathroom, Gloria saw a hundred million Glorias
reflected in the mirrors. She saw a hundred
million Missys, too. She and Missy grew tiny
far back in the mirrors. When she moved her
head, all the girls in the mirrors did, too.
When she lifted Missy's hand in a wave, all
the dolls in the mirror waved back.

Gloria ran her fingertips over the shiny
gold tiles of the countertop. "This could be
a skating rink for you, Missy." She put her
finger in the center of the pile of tiny, lacy
towels and pushed down, then watched the
towels rise back up when she took her finger
away.

Mama wheeled a cart of cleaning supplies and a mop bucket. "I'll start the toilets, Gloria. You can help me by wiping out those sinks."

She handed Gloria a rag, then wound up her braid and pinned it into a fat bun at the back of her head.

Gloria moved the rag very slowly. She and Missy were princesses trapped in the enchanted mirrors.

Mama put the toilet brush back in a bucket. Then she mopped the floor and set up a yellow plastic sign that said WET FLOORS.

"There's something else you can do, Gloria." Mama beckoned her inside a toilet stall. "See the end of the toilet paper? I'm folding it into a triangle. Like this. I'll get the mirrors polished while you make the toilet paper look pretty."

Gloria looked at Mama to see if she was joking. She expected Mama to start giggling and give her a hug until they were both laughing together. Then she would say, "Oh,

Gloria. Let's go on home now and forget this silliness."

But Mama wasn't smiling as she reached for the blue spray bottle on the top of the cart.

Gloria went into each stall and folded the toilet paper, the tissue thin and slippery between her fingers. "But Mama," she protested after the third stall, "the first time anyone goes in here, the paper will look just like it did before."

"That's why I'm here all day, *mija*."

"*To fold toilet paper?*" Gloria couldn't believe she was missing Christmas so Mama could do something so useless.

"And to give each guest a towel and to clean up the water that drips on the counters."

"But can't the bathroom be a little messy on Christmas?"

"Especially not on Christmas."

Gloria looked at the pile of towels. One for each guest to use once? At home, Mama made her use her bath towel for a whole week.

"I have to hurry, Gloria. The guests will soon stop in on their way to eat."

Mama put a silver tray in the middle of the gold tiles.

"What's that for?" Gloria asked. The tray looked as though it should be full of candies.

"For tips, *mija*. That's where all the change that I bring home in my purse every night comes from. I stand right here." Mama went to a corner and folded her hands in front of her. "Each lady will put a quarter in the tray. Sometimes they'll look at my name tag and say, 'Thank you, Marta,' as they go out."

"Maybe they'll eat breakfast quickly and go home so we can go, too."

Mama laughed. "No, this meal is called *brunch*—breakfast and lunch combined. It's a fancy meal that goes on all day."

That sounded good to Gloria. Her breakfast of cold cereal was all burned up. While Mama tidied the bathroom, Gloria filled a sink. "This is the pool but there's no seals." She took off

Missy's socks and shoes and dipped her plastic feet into the water.

"Gloria, please. See all the splashes you've made on the mirror?" Mama took a paper towel and polished the drops away.

Gloria peeked out the door and saw Santa coming out of the men's bathroom, adjusting his belt around his fat stomach. "Hey, I'm right here!" Gloria called loudly. But he didn't look over.

"It's ten o'clock, Gloria. Almost time for you to leave." Mama tapped her watch with a clean pinkish fingernail.

Just then a woman in a red dress came in. She clicked across the clean floor with her high heels and went into a stall.

"Let's go," Mama whispered.

They walked into a big room where the crystal lights made rainbows all over the walls. "Wow!" Gloria stopped. It was just like *Unicorns under a Rainbow*, one of her favorite TV shows.

Everywhere she looked, she saw something

that made her heart beat faster. This place made the beach look like hardly any fun at all! "Look, Missy! Just your size." She held her doll up toward a sleigh like the one Santa rode in, except this one was carved out of ice. The ice dripped onto plates loaded with bunches of grapes, melon scooped into perfect balls, and pineapple triangles.

As she and Mama walked down the long table, they passed steaming trays of eggs and crispy hash browns cooked just the way Gloria liked them best, whole turkeys waiting to be cut. So this was where she'd spend Christmas! She wanted to reach out and hug Mama.

Gloria gasped. There was a piano on top of the food table! A man wearing a Santa hat was fooling around, not playing any songs yet, because no guests had come, just making happy little notes. Gloria wanted to ask him how he got up there without stepping in the plates of sliced cheese.

When they arrived at the end of the table,

Gloria reached for a piece of cake with sparkly icing. Mama grabbed her wrist. *"Gloria!"*

They had come to the end of the room, but Mama kept marching on.

"Mama, where are we going?" Gloria walked quickly to catch up.

"To the kitchen, *mija.*"

"I'm not going to stay *here?*"

Mama looked down at her, her face blank for a moment. Then she shook her head. "You don't understand, Gloria. All this," she gestured toward the room, "is for the guests."

"But, *Mama* . . ." Gloria's body shrank back into itself.

Mama knelt down in front of Gloria and tried to bring her into a hug. But Gloria pulled back and made her body stiff all over.

Mama sighed. "Come, *mija.*"

When Mama pushed open the doors to the kitchen, Gloria saw only pasty white walls. No Christmas tree or any decorations at all. The strips of white lights overhead made everything look plain.

Right beyond the doors was a huge counter where several women, their hair bound in nets, were chopping vegetables. At home, Mama liked to hum tunes as she cut vegetables for salads or soups. These women chopped in silence, bringing the knives up and down swiftly over the carrots, celery, and round heads of lettuce. Their mouths looked determined not to sing a note.

Mama went around the back of the salad counter, leading Gloria by the hand. She spoke to one of the women. "This is Gloria, Carmen. I had to bring her with me. Would you be able to watch her?"

The woman glanced at Gloria and nodded, but didn't stop hacking away with her knife. "*Está bien,*" that's fine, she said.

Mama turned to Gloria. "Carmen will watch you." Mama pushed Gloria's shopping bag of presents under the counter. She helped Gloria onto a tall stool.

Gloria looked around the kitchen. On the other side of the salad counter she saw a line of stoves and a row of men in white hats stirring and flipping food. Gloria smelled meat and vegetables and desserts all mixed together. Unlike the silent women, the men yelled back and forth. Gloria wanted to cover her ears. She hoped that none of the cooks would yell at her.

"I'd rather be with you, Mama." At least she could wait in the bathroom with the mirrors and gold tiles.

"Oh, no, Gloria. Grown-up ladies don't want to see a little girl in the bathroom."

"But I wouldn't bother anyone, Mama. I'd play with Missy."

Mama shook her head. She knelt down again but didn't touch Gloria. "The owners might find out that you're here," she whispered. "Don't worry. I'll check on you at lunchtime."

"But—" Gloria slipped off the stool.

"Bye, Gloria. Be good," said Mama as she pushed open the swinging door.

CHAPTER 5

Radishes and Roses

"Stay away from the big pots, little one. They're hot. And when the waiters come through, keep out of their way. See that break room on the other side of the stoves?" Carmen gestured with the knife, pointing with the tip. "Hide in there if a guy in a suit comes in. That's the boss."

Gloria stood near Carmen, just out of range of her elbows as she chopped. Her knife *thwack thwacked* on the big wooden board. Over and over, Carmen lifted the carrots and celery into the bowl.

A young man wheeled a load of clean dishes on a cart through the swinging doors into the dining room. He came back with the cart piled high with dirty dishes. He was so tall that he had to bend over to grab the cart's handles. He whistled "Jingle Bells."

"Hey, Ricardo, cut it with the merry, merry stuff, would ya?" a cook shouted as Ricardo crossed the kitchen.

"Yeah, I'm not feeling exactly Christmasy," said another.

Me neither, thought Gloria.

A man began to load Ricardo's dirty plates and silverware onto racks. When he squirted the racks with water, that part of the kitchen filled with such thick steam that Gloria could see nothing but the man's bright yellow gloves.

Ricardo reached up to the shelf for another stack of dishes. As he turned back to the cart, he glanced down at Gloria. He smiled and made a motion as though he were going to toss the dishes in the direction of the complaining cooks.

Gloria couldn't help but smile back.

Missy was getting bored with the vegetable

chopping, so Gloria moved toward the door into the dining room. The door swung open as Ricardo passed through. In that moment, Santa Claus came by with a bag of candy on his back. "Ho, ho, ho," he said softly and tucked a lollipop into Gloria's hand.

Gloria stood by the swinging doors, waiting for them to open again. When they did, she and Missy stepped through the doors to meet Santa. This time instead of giving them candy, he made a little shooing motion toward the kitchen with his white-gloved hand.

Gloria moved back, out of the dining room. But beyond Santa Claus, she had seen a girl her own age sitting at a table with her family. When Santa had passed, Gloria opened the swinging door just a crack. The girl had long even curls the color of butterscotch candy.

Mama said that Gloria's long hair was the color of chocolate.

The girl laughed suddenly. She jerked her fork and a bite of strawberry pie spilled on her lacy dress.

The girl's mother leaned forward to brush at the spill with a napkin.

The girl offered a bite of whipped cream to the fluffy stuffed dog sitting next to her on the chair.

"That could be us," Gloria said to Missy. Her tummy gave a growl.

Carmen led Gloria to a stool by the work table. "I've got a job for you, *mija*." She placed a platter of chopped ice in front of Gloria—*a mountain of snow,* Gloria said silently to Missy—then a bowlful of radishes floating in water.

When Gloria looked closely, she saw that the radishes had been cut so that they looked like flowers. "How did you do that?" she asked Carmen.

"Like this." Carmen took a knife and made quick slices around the outside of a radish, forming the petals.

"Can I try that?" Gloria asked.

"No. You can't use the knife. But you can arrange the finished ones on the ice."

As Gloria set the radish roses on the platter, she found one with a broken petal.

"Don't worry," Carmen said. "People just pop these in their mouths. They don't look closely. Mostly, they don't eat them at all."

It was true that Ricardo's dirty dishes returned with a lot of radish roses. Now when he came back and forth with his cart, he didn't sing anything.

When Gloria had finished, she held the platter up to Carmen.

"Okay. Very nice. Now do me a favor. Just slip into the dining room for a quick second and slide those right next to the celery sticks. Come right back."

Gloria set Missy on the stool, then lifted the plate carefully with both hands.

Ricardo opened the swinging doors for her, and just like that she was in the dining room.

The lights glinted from all directions. People laughed and talked over the tinkly piano music, and the good smells of the food mixed together.

In between the plates of celery sticks and

carrot sticks rested a plate with one radish rose. Gloria was setting down her platter when she heard a voice.

"Oooh, those are pretty." It was the girl with the lacy dress. She stood next to Gloria, just Gloria's height. She smelled sweet, like Gloria's coconut shampoo. When the girl reached toward the platter, Gloria noticed that her ring had a red heart-shaped stone. The girl picked up a radish rose.

"I made them myself," Gloria said, surprising herself. She hardly ever fibbed.

The girl examined the radish rose. The lace collar of her dress was threaded all around with red and green ribbon. "How?"

"With a knife."

"A real knife?"

"Not a long one. About like this." Gloria held her fingers a little apart. Then she moved them a little more apart to make Carmen's knife seem a teeny bit longer than it really was.

The girl held the fluffy white dog under her arm.

Gloria longed to touch the fur. "What's her name?" she asked, looking at the dog.

"Stuffy," the girl replied.

Gloria was glad that she'd left Missy in the kitchen. It was okay to have a stuffed animal— even teenagers had those—but some girls thought that dolls were for little kids.

"I got her for Christmas," the girl continued.

Gloria looked at Stuffy. She wondered if the girl would mind if she touched the dog just once on the front paws. She reached her hand out. "Could I . . . ?"

"Of course."

The dog's fur felt drier and stiffer than it looked. Gloria petted the paws, then the top of the head, stroking the fur so that it flattened under her palm.

The girl leaned close, as though she were telling a special secret. She smiled at Gloria as though she were her new best friend. "I also got some Rollerblades and colored pencils that you dip into water and they're just like paint, the bedspread with roses that I'd been wanting with curtains to match, and this necklace." She pointed to the tiny pearls that circled her throat. "And when we get home and Grandma and Grandpa Barrett come over they're going to bring more presents. I think they got me a helmet and knee pads to go with the Rollerblades." The girl took a step backward, as though to judge Gloria's reaction.

Gloria stared. The lights seemed to swirl around her. She had never heard of anyone getting so much at once. Last year at the beach she'd gotten only the camera.

"What about you?" the girl asked. "What did you get?"

Gloria considered. She could lie, but she didn't know where to begin. Because she'd never dreamed of having so many things, she couldn't even name them. "We haven't celebrated yet. We do that tonight. At Grandma Santamaria's house."

"Then what are you doing here?"

Gloria could feel the girl looking her up

and down. What was the girl looking at? Suddenly she felt a warm feeling rise from her neck into her cheeks.

"I'm waiting for Mama. She's in the bath-room."

"But she'll come out soon. Then you can eat lunch."

"She's not using the bathroom. She's clean-ing it." Right away Gloria knew she'd said the wrong thing.

"Like a *maid*, you mean?" The girl hugged Stuffy.

Gloria turned to see if anyone in the dining room had heard the word that the girl almost shouted. Not only was Mama a maid, but Sandra's mom was, too. She thought of other girls from her class at school. Maria Isabella's mother did rooms at the Heidy Ho Inn on G Street. Ana's mom worked as a waitress, which was almost the same thing. All the moms were good moms. Yet this girl had said *maid* as though it were a bad word.

A woman in a sequined black dress leaned

in to gather olives and cheese slices, using the silver tongs to lift them onto her plate.

"What does your mother do?" Gloria asked after the woman had moved on.

"My mom . . . " the girl began. She rolled her eyes toward the ceiling of sparkling lights, as though searching for the answer. "My mom doesn't do anything."

"Nothing?"

"Nothing much except take care of me."

Gloria was glad that the girl hadn't said anything about her father. She was afraid that the girl would say her dad was a prince or a king. Or maybe he was so rich he did nothing at all. She thought of Papi working on Christmas. Right now he was ripping bright oranges one by one from their branches, throwing each over his shoulder into a basket strapped on his back.

Thinking of Papi, Gloria knocked her elbow against the plate of radish roses. She turned to see the plate teeter for a second on the edge of the table. Then the radishes tumbled soundlessly, in little clumps, onto the soft pink carpet.

Gloria and the girl both covered their mouths. They looked at each other and giggled, then knelt on all fours to pick up the radishes.

"This is like hunting Easter eggs," said the girl, crawling out from under the food table. She handed Gloria three radish roses.

Gloria suddenly saw the girl's mom watching her. Something in the mom's face made Gloria recall finding the broken radish rose and wondering whether she should throw it out.

"Sylvie!"

The girl looked up and pushed her hair back from her face. "Yes, Mom?"

"You'll ruin your dress."

Sylvie stood and pulled the ruffles straight on her sleeves, holding her dog under first one arm, then the other. She looked down at Gloria, paused, then put Stuffy in Gloria's arms. "Take her. Grandma Barrett said we should give to the have-nots."

As Sylvie walked back to her family she turned and waved at Gloria.

Gloria waved too—a tiny movement with just her fingers.

Holding Stuffy in one arm, Gloria lifted the plate of radish roses back onto the table. Some had bits of pink rug stuck in the petals. But as Carmen said, no one ever ate them anyway.

CHAPTER 6

The Back Way

"Where'd that come from?" Carmen asked, stopping her work to glance at Stuffy.

"A girl gave her to me."

"So that's why you were gone so long. Don't go mixing with the guests, or we'll all be in hot water."

Gloria sat down in a chair near a small window. Outside, she could see the bright blue ocean, the tops of the feathery palms, and a turquoise swimming pool the color of Sylvie's eyes. She set Missy aside on the counter and hugged Stuffy tight.

"We're going to run away," Gloria whispered into Stuffy's ear. "We'll get ourselves adopted by a mother who doesn't have to work on Christmas. Our new mother will bring us to eat in the dining room, not make us watch from the kitchen."

She puzzled over the words *have-not*. Did it mean that she didn't have something? Didn't have what? Didn't have *anything*? Next to Sylvie, she seemed to have nothing.

The word *maid* rang out over and over in Gloria's mind.

A smell of something burning spread throughout the kitchen, and one of the cooks yelled louder than usual.

Ricardo wheeled in a new stack of dirty plates. On the top sat a plate of roast beef and mashed potatoes that someone hadn't eaten.

"Hungry?" Ricardo held the plate out to Gloria. He smiled, showing a flash of gold tooth. "It's lunchtime. No one's touched it. I was watching."

Gloria longed to turn away and tell him: *I want my own plate!*

But she let him set the food in front of her. He brought her a clean fork. The roast beef broke easily into bites. The mashed potatoes tasted like a buttery cloud. She gobbled it all down.

When Missy had to go pee, Carmen showed Gloria the kitchen bathroom. It had a plain toilet and sink. "Look, Missy. Ordinary toilet paper. No one folded the end into a triangle for *us*!" Gloria wanted to leave the bathroom without using it. She felt like slamming the door hard behind her as she left.

๏๛๏

When the clock on the wall said two o'clock, Mama came into the kitchen, pushing through one side of the double door. "Ai, *mijita,* you must be hungry." She pulled Gloria against her with one arm.

But Gloria leaned away from Mama instead of snuggling into her pink uniform that was losing its starch.

"What a cute doggie. Where did you get it?"

Gloria turned away and pressed her face into Stuffy's dry fur.

"What have you been doing today?" Mama asked, as if nothing were wrong.

Gloria shrugged.

"Ready, Marta?" the cook named Sammy called out. When Mama nodded, Gloria watched Sammy peel paper off a thin hamburger patty and lay the meat on the grill.

"I have good news for you, Gloria," Mama said, sitting down on a stool next to her. "Regine, my boss, likes the way I keep the bathroom so nice. This morning she said to me, 'Marta, when they move me up, maybe you can take my job.'"

"So?" said Gloria, kicking the rungs of the stool.

"So I'd get paid a little more."

Sammy set a hamburger and a handful of chips down in front of Mama. "Sorry I can't give you two. They count these patties."

Mama began to cut the hamburger in half.

"I don't want any of that nasty meat," Gloria said. "I already had fancy food."

Mama stopped cutting. For a moment, the

corners of her mouth tightened. Then she said, "I'm glad you had a nice lunch."

Gloria watched Mama eat. Mama looked so hurried taking the small quick bites, wiping the drips of ketchup from the edges of her mouth with a napkin. Gloria thought of Sylvie's mom talking and laughing in between bites, taking all the time in the world to eat.

Mama carried her plate to the stack to be washed. "Only a few more hours, Gloria," she called. She lifted her fingers and blew a kiss across the kitchen.

Gloria turned her cheek away just as the kiss would have landed.

❧

"I have another job for you," Carmen said after Mama left. She led Gloria to a place where a woman was slicing turkey and arranging it on platters. "I've got you a helper, Fran."

Fran hardly looked up. "I been wrestling with these big guys all day, kid," she said, patting a turkey on the breast. "I'm too tired to

47

chitchat." Fran handed Gloria a clean white towel. "See these platters? See how the gravy spilled here on the edge? I need you to wipe that off before they go out to the dining room."

Gloria wiped one platter after another as Fran made them ready. She turned her face away whenever the kitchen doors swung open. She was sure that Sylvie was gone. But she didn't want any other rich girls to see her cleaning gravy off platters.

Carmen came by with a bowl of lettuce. "Your mama should be coming soon. She says you're going to your nana's house."

Nana's house. She had almost forgotten. Nana's house suddenly seemed small, unimportant, and very far away.

❦

Just as the sun was dipping into the ocean outside the small window, Mama came into the kitchen. "Time to go, Gloria," she said. Even though her name tag was crooked and her hair was coming loose from her bun, she

almost sang the words, as though Christmas weren't already practically over.

Mama got Gloria's shopping bag out from under the counter, then reached into her pocket and pulled out some coins. Carmen was washing dishes. When she saw Mama, she pulled one hand out of the soapy water. Gloria heard the coins go *clink clink* as they passed from Mama's hand to Carmen's.

"She was no trouble, none at all," said Carmen. "Bye, *mija. ¡Feliz Navidad!*"

"You, too," Gloria mumbled. She couldn't make herself say the words *Merry Christmas*.

<hr>

"This time," Mama said as they walked through the kitchen, "we have to go out the back way."

"But we came in the front."

"I know, Gloria. We shouldn't have. I wanted you to see the big tree."

"So why can't I see it again?" Gloria asked as they began to walk down flights of gray linoleum steps. The staircase was quiet after the noisy kitchen.

"There's too many guests. They might see us."

"So?"

Mama paused as though she were thinking, then continued slowly. "We're here to make Christmas nice for the guests. It's not our place to be among them."

CHAPTER 7

Lights from Two Countries

Outside at the dark bus stop, Gloria tucked Missy and Stuffy underneath her sweater.

At Sandra's, the party would just be getting started on the patio, the lights strung along the roof all plugged in and twinkling. The piñata would be so full of candies that the tree branch would hang low. A CD might be playing on the boom box, or maybe Sandra's uncle Eddie was strumming his electric guitar and singing songs. On party nights, people danced in and out between the old cars. The men wore tight dark clothes, but the women wore party dresses, the loose skirts like clusters of flower petals. As night fell, the laughter would get louder and sillier.

But even Sandra's party, Gloria thought, was nothing compared to Christmas at the hotel.

Mostly, Gloria thought about Sylvie. Maybe she was opening more presents with her Grandma and Grandpa Barrett. Maybe she was Rollerblading or falling asleep under her new bedspread, dreaming of roses. Sylvie's mama did nothing at all. Her mama was definitely not a maid.

"We'll be at Nana's soon," Mama said.

Gloria hardly cared. When the bus came she planned to make a pillow out of Stuffy, fall asleep, and forget Christmas.

❦

The Number 23 bus went to the border. Everyone had to get off near the large archway.

"This is America, Gloria," Mama put one foot on the sidewalk as she always did, "and this is Mexico." She put down her other foot on concrete just inches away. "I'm standing in two countries."

Usually when Mama did that, Gloria liked

to hop back and forth, chanting a little song she'd made up to the tune of "Twinkle, Twinkle, Little Star": *Mexico, U.S.A., I-can-hop-from-you-to-you.*

But tonight, she just sighed.

Instead of the shiny, gray bus with its bright lights, Gloria and Mama caught a dark green *camión*. The bus was dented all over and Gloria thought it looked like the way she felt. All the seats were taken, so they had to stand, holding onto a pole.

A man held a baby who cried no matter which way he held her. Finally, the man placed a piece of hard candy against the baby's lips. Every time the bus swayed and Gloria rocked forward toward the man, Gloria smelled the strong peppermint.

The man left at the first stop, and Mama pushed Gloria quickly into the empty seat.

Next to her sat a boy with a tray of Chiclets strapped around his shoulders. He stared straight ahead into the gray plastic of the seat in front of him. He'd probably roamed the

streets all day selling the chewing gum. It didn't look as though *he* was having a good Christmas either. In fact, it looked as if he was having a worse Christmas than Gloria.

For a moment, Gloria considered giving Stuffy to the boy. He might have a sister who was even more of a have-not than Gloria was. But when she imagined handing over Stuffy, she also imagined the hole she'd be left with. Stuffy had made such a warm spot where she'd pressed her against her chest. Gloria buried her face in Stuffy's fur and held her tighter.

Hanging by a string from the driver's mirror, the Virgin Mary jiggled up and down as the bus bounced over potholes, through the city, and into the hillsides along the dirt roads.

Instead of just reaching up to yank a wire when they got to Nana's street, Mama had to push her way to the front of the bus. *"Señor."* She tapped the driver on the shoulder.

They got out at a corner where a man sold tacos in a little stand. The bare lightbulb hanging from the stand shone on barrels filled with yellow and pink drinks and on the rocky path that led up the hill. A cold breeze caught Gloria around the ankles. She shivered and pushed her face into Missy's hair.

Nana's *colonia* had no electricity. There weren't real houses like the one that Gloria lived in. Candlelight and kerosene lamps shone from within shelters made of cardboard and blue tarps. Bonfires burned here and there all the way up the hill.

When Gloria stubbed her toe on a rock in the dirt road, she stumbled and dropped Missy. Mama found her and tucked her into Gloria's arms. Gloria had to bite Missy's plastic fingers to keep from crying.

At the top of the hill, they reached Nana's house.

"Look, Gloria, city lights from two countries. What a view your Nana has!"

Gloria glanced over the hillsides. The lights looked like diamonds, rubies, and emeralds— the birthstones sold at the checkout counter at

Save-a-Lot. Somewhere down there, sparkling and twinkling, was Mama's hotel.

Nana had made *luminarios* by putting sand inside of paper bags and standing candles in the sand. With the candles lit and burning all around, Nana's house looked pretty, not like a place made of scraps of wood.

When Nana opened the door, she was lit from behind by more candles. *"¡Feliz Navidad!"* she said. While Nana hugged Mama, Gloria peeked into Nana's one-room house. No Papi and no place for him to hide.

Nana reached down for Gloria, her smile softening at the edges. *"Ai, niñita."* Nana had eyes so dark they looked black. Nana had a long braid like Mama's coiled around her head like a crown.

Gloria pressed her face against Nana's woolly scarf that smelled of herbs. She wouldn't let herself cry. Or Missy either.

"Gloria has had a long day at work with me," Mama said.

"And on Christmas, too. *Pobrecita.*"

Gloria wiped her cheeks on Nana's scarf. She hoped that Nana didn't see.

"Who is this?" Nana held Stuffy in both hands.

"Stuffy," said Gloria.

"*Stoofy,*" repeated Nana with her accent.

Nana took Gloria's hand and led her over to the Nativity. "*Gloria.* That's what the shepherds said when they saw the baby. You have a special name, *mija.*"

On a round table, Nana had set up the wooden manger on a bed of straw. Shepherds and wise men stood to the side. Tucked inside the manger, surrounded by cows and sheep, the Virgin Mary and Joseph knelt before the baby in his cradle. Nana never minded if Gloria took the figures out of the manger and played with them. Gloria was always careful to put them back exactly as she'd found them. But tonight she didn't feel like playing.

Candles stood dark in tall red and green glass jars, ready to be lit after dinner. Everyone knelt to light a candle, then to sing, their shoulders touching, their faces glowing. Every year, Gloria looked forward to the tradition that honored the baby Jesus.

Gloria watched Mama put the shopping bag near the Nativity. She didn't even care about giving the gifts anymore. She felt as though an ice cube had gotten stuck in her throat and refused to melt.

Mama emptied the coins from her purse. She took one of Nana's hands, opened it, and poured the quarters and dimes into it. She closed Nana's fingers over the coins. Nana shook her head "no" but Mama held Nana's hand in a fist until she gave up.

Nana unscrewed the lid on a big jar and dropped the coins in with others. "Come help me, Gloria," Nana called. "Let your mama rest a minute."

The table was set with a bright red cloth. Three white plates shone in the light from the kerosene lamp. Nana handed Gloria bowls of rice and beans, and a flat round container of tortillas. Nana had just steamed the tortillas, and the moist warmth came through the plastic.

"Something special for Christmas, Gloria." Nana lifted the lid of a small pot. A delicious steam rose from the *carne seca.* Nana had shredded the dried meat, then cooked it with oregano, garlic, and green chile.

"Ready now, Marta?" Nana asked Mama, who had just put her feet up and closed her eyes.

They sat down at the table with their sweaters still on. Gloria could almost see her breath, the air was so cold, even inside.

"How was work?" Nana asked Mama.

"Not too bad. It was fun to see the pretty dresses the ladies wore."

Fun! How could Mama use such a word? Every bit had been horrible.

Gloria peeled off the steaming husk of her tamale, then plunged her fork into the layers of soft corn filled with meat and olives.

"Did you make the tamales with Elena again?" Mama asked.

"Oh yes. We had quite a party. Six of us took turns stirring the corn meal. Blanca cooked the filling. Esmeralda wrapped the filling into the corn. I wrapped the tamales in the husks."

As Gloria ate the familiar foods, her stomach grew warm. She unbuttoned her sweater and leaned back in her chair. Missy and Stuffy weren't crying anymore. *If I'd never been to Mama's hotel, I'd be feeling happy right now,* Gloria thought.

For dessert, Nana brought out hot chocolate with cinnamon floating on top and *camote,* candied yams that she'd bought at the taco stand at the bottom of the hill.

"Pass these to your tired mama," Nana said, handing Gloria a small dish of tamarind candies, dark and sweet and spiced with chile.

As Gloria passed the dish, she thought of how the candies were a part of every holiday and birthday. Nana saw to that. She either stuffed them into a piñata or served them in a little bowl with hot chiles painted around the rim.

The people fixing food at Mama's hotel had been tired and grumpy. No one seemed to care about adding loving touches for the sake of the strangers in the fancy dining room. But Nana had worked for days to make Christmas dinner special.

CHAPTER 8

Feliz Navidad

Nana heated water on the stove and poured it into the plastic dishwashing tub. As she washed each dish, she handed it to Gloria to dry.

Gloria swirled the rag around and around. Here she was in another kitchen, but worse than the last. This kitchen was small and dark. The stove had only two burners, and Nana didn't even have a normal refrigerator. It was a big old one, and Nana had nowhere to plug it in. Every other day a man came by with a block of ice to put inside.

As Gloria handed Mama the dry forks and plates, she made sure that her fingers never touched Mama's. It was Mama's fault that Christmas was ruined.

Mama stacked the clean dishes on Nana's orange crate shelves.

"I want you to quit that job!" Gloria suddenly said.

Nana put her hand on Gloria's shoulder so heavily that she had to stop wiping. "Her job takes care of both of us." Nana's voice was firm. Her black eyes looked straight into Gloria's.

Gloria turned her face away. "There's other places where they don't make you work on Christmas. I saw lots of stores closed today."

Nana knelt down beside Gloria. "Listen, *mija*. We're all here together now. We love you with our big hearts." She took Gloria's hand and placed it over her chest. "Feel my heart beating just for you."

Gloria felt a dull thud under Nana's sweater.

Mama came close. "You know you're special to us. We want you to have a nice Christmas with us." She pointed to herself and then to Nana.

"Papi's not here."

Mama sighed. "He couldn't help it."

"The girl said I was a have-not," said Gloria.

"The girl who gave you the dog?" Mama asked.

"She said you were a what?" asked Nana.

"Someone who has nothing."

"But you have us, Gloria. How can you be a have-not?"

Gloria didn't say anything. Ever since she'd seen the hotel and met Sylvie, what had once been plenty now wasn't enough.

"I know what would make us all feel better," said Nana. "Let's open your presents." She led Gloria to her bed against the wall. "You and your mama can get cozy."

Nana brought out a package wrapped in newspaper.

When Gloria tore it open, she found clothes for Missy: three dresses, a blouse, and a sparkly party skirt. Nana had sewn them out of scraps.

"These are for Missy's bed." Mama handed Gloria pieces of soft white fabric.

Gloria recognized the tiny towels from the hotel bathroom.

"I mended the torn ones they threw away," Mama said.

Gloria took the towels from Mama.

"Why are you looking so sad, Gloria?" Mama asked.

"I'm not."

"You wanted to enjoy the pretty hotel," Mama said.

"Well yes, if I had to *be* there."

"Are you crying, Gloria?" Mama asked.

Teardrops glistened on Stuffy's fur. Gloria covered her face with her hands and shook her head.

"You have one more present, Gloria." Nana touched Gloria's shoulder. "Your Papi left me something to give you."

Gloria peeked from between her fingers. What could Papi have left?

Nana held out a small book.

Mama and Nana drew close as Gloria opened the book in the dim light. In spite of herself, her heart lit up: inside were the pictures from the beach last Christmas! Each photograph was carefully protected by a sleeve of clear, slippery plastic.

Even though Papi was away, he'd remembered her!

As Gloria turned the pages, she saw the waves, the sand castle, the dancing fire, and Nana, Papi, and Mama, over and over.

There was Papi holding a stick with marshmallows over the fire, his curly hair blowing wildly in the wind.

"I forgot, Marta, how you wore that wreath of seaweed around your head," said Nana, touching a picture lightly.

There was the big wave crashing over the sand castle, leaving the tallest tower in a soft, shapeless mound.

When she came to the last image of all, Mama, Nana, and Papi posing together with big smiles, Gloria turned back to the front and looked through the photos again.

"Gloria." Mama laid a hand on Gloria's arm.

"New Year's Day is coming up. . . ."

"Or there's always Three Kings' Day," said Nana.

"Could we go to the beach then?" asked Gloria, her voice like a shadow.

"We can hope," Mama answered.

After they'd examined the pictures carefully for the third time, Gloria's heart felt warm. Papi had taken time to make a gift for her. Mama and Nana had made clothes and blankets for Missy. They did love her with big hearts.

Gloria snuggled into the warm space between Mama and Nana, but she didn't dare look either of them in the eyes. All day long she had been confused about Christmas. To think she had thought the hotel was better than this!

Gloria remembered then that she hadn't given her gifts. She crossed the room and took the shopping bag by both handles.

First, she lifted out the angel in its nest of tissue paper.

When Nana unwrapped the angel, her face looked surprised, just the way that Gloria had imagined. She turned the angel around and around, looking at it from all sides. "How did you ever make this?" she exclaimed.

Gloria explained how she'd formed the angel out of soft red clay, and how her teacher had taken it to be fired in a special oven.

Nana took the angel to the Nativity and set it by the baby Jesus. It stood perfectly, without wobbling a bit.

Gloria gave Mama the plaster-of-paris hand.

"Oh, Gloria." Mama took Gloria's real hand and pressed it against the plaster form. "This will always help me remember how you looked when you were nine years old." She took Gloria's real hand again and kissed the palm.

Gloria held up the pinecone with its glitter. "This is Papi's."

"A New Year's gift," said Mama.

"Or a Three Kings' gift," said Nana.

It was time for the candle-lighting tradition. They knelt in front of the candles surrounding the Nativity. Nana lit her candle first, then Mama lit hers. When Mama was finished, she handed the long match to Gloria, who lit her own candle and Papi's.

When all the candles were aflame, red and green light danced over the tiny people and animals in the Nativity.

Mama and Nana began to sing, their voices blending together, "*Esta Noche es Nochebuena.*" They sang about how the Holy Night was the night of the fiery red flowers like the ones that Gloria had seen growing around the palm trees at the hotel. *Night of the moon and night of the stars. . . .*

Gloria's voice came out a little shaky, like the flame of her heart.

After the song, Gloria said quietly, "I think I'll dress Missy in her new clothes now."

"What a good idea." Nana gave her a hug around the waist.

Gloria lifted her face to Mama and smiled. "Missy loves her pretty new blankets. She will share them with Stuffy."

✸

When the candles had burned down in their

glasses and the smell of hot wax filled the house, Mama said, "I have to work tomorrow, too. It's time to go."

Gloria stretched under her blanket. Nana's house was so cozy that she'd almost fallen asleep.

Nana kissed them good-bye and handed Gloria a brown bag full of warm tamales. "For tomorrow."

"Thank you, Nana. Merry Christmas after all." Gloria hugged Nana, breathing in the scent of her scarf. "Missy and Stuffy are saying *Feliz Navidad*, too," she whispered.

Outside, the candles in Nana's *luminarios* had burned down, leaving her front yard in darkness.

But the lights of the two countries still sparkled and twinkled below.

"What a view my Nana has!" said Gloria, taking Mama's hand.

Gloria held Mama's hand tightly as they walked toward the lights, down the steep hill.